Nothing New Under the Sun

To my sweet Godfather
and his lovely wife!

Fabienne Brush
August 24, 2009

Nothing New Under the Sun

◆

A Journey from Atheism to Faith

Fabienne Brush

iUniverse, Inc.
New York Lincoln Shanghai

Nothing New Under the Sun
A Journey from Atheism to Faith

iUniverse, Inc.

For information address:
iUniverse, Inc.
2021 Pine Lake Road, Suite 100
Lincoln, NE 68512
www.iuniverse.com

ISBN: 0-595-28420-5

Printed in the United States of America

…Dedicated to the gentle people of Okinawa, Japan;
Whose warm hospitality was my inspiration;
And to all people of every nation, whom God calls for His own…

Contents

Foreword

The old words of wisdom are certainly true. There is nothing new under the sun. Each person, during the course of his or her life, has 'revelations' which seem unique to his own psyche, but which somewhere, sometime, more than likely, have already been conceived. So, what is revealed in this book is not a lightning bolt out of the sky, but leads the lost down the same path to faith others have followed since time began.

The reader is not berated with statistics to 'prove' God's existence. Only the most dedicated would plow through all that, and if not convinced of the argument in the first place, would probably abandon in the first chapter. Rather, a series of obvious facts are offered, in succeeding order, much like the progressive steps in proving a hypothesis.

Most atheists claim to be enlightened and open-minded. If the reader adheres to this premise, he is challenged to read this book devoid of preconceived notions or forgone conclusions. This step-by-step process does take a logical progression. At some point, however, that leap of faith must be taken, in order to believe in something one cannot see, hear, smell, taste, or feel with the physical senses.

How, then, does one come to terms with this concept of belief, when so many other philosophical ideas are floating around? Certainly, most intelligent people do conceive of a world beyond the physical; but is it real? And if it is real, what is it all about? How can one sift through all the chaff and get to the wheat?

An evolution of thought leads the soul to reach its full fruition. No human being is completely fulfilled until he returns spiritually to his Creator, and lives in harmony with Him. There is a persistent inner longing that nothing else will satisfy...

1

Is There a God?

An atheist believes there is no god. Assuming the person is intelligent, he or she must have reached this conclusion by way of critical thinking. The usual logic comes from the, "If I can't hear, see, touch, smell, or feel it, it doesn't exist," attitude. Another is, "If there is a loving god, why is there so much suffering in the world?" This type of person is very literal, obviously, and therefore must be persuaded only by deductive reasoning. This is not a criticism in any way of the atheist, rather a compliment. Only a fool puts his trust in fluff!

It follows, then, that if there is no god, then everything is strictly physical. Science, logic, and nature can be trusted. These things are tangible, explainable, and can be proven, or if not, can at least be theorized based on some kind of evidence. The atheist is now left with two basic questions to solve. What are the origin and meaning of life?

Most often, the atheist believes the theory of evolution, rather than the creation story. The theory of evolution, in very simple terms, is this: The earth began with a cosmic 'big bang' and evolved over billions of years to the point that it could support life. Then, some existent chemicals got mixed in pond water, which brought forth some type of simple life form. This evolved into higher life forms, in order to survive in different situations. Some of these crawled out onto the sand and evolved into some things that could be sustained by air rather than water, and so on, until we humans arrived as the utmost of life forms.

The creation story is the traditional biblical one. It begins with God creating the earth in six days, resting on the seventh (no one knows how long a day is to God), and culminates with the creation of Man, or Adam, and later Eve, in the Garden of Eden.

On first impression, anyone listening to these two points of view would probably lean toward evolution. But if deductive reasoning is applied and the theories are fully explored, the final conclusion might be different.

Let us first examine the evolution theory. What are the chances of some existent chemicals coming together to form something that lives, breathes, eats, procreates, voids, ages, and finally dies? Could random circumstances so perfectly align so as to bring about such ends? From a common sense standpoint alone the probability of the two chemicals randomly coming together in water and forming life is astronomical. Add to that a few more particulars. For example, what is the probability of the earth becoming aligned with the sun and moon in such a way as to produce just the right conditions to allow life to exist? Did you know that the earth rotates on its average twenty-three degrees axis only because of the position and size of our moon? And, if not for the moon, the rotation would slow and wobble to a point that our climate would be inconsistent, chaotic, and unable to sustain life. Consider that air, water, temperature, sustenance, resources, and the list goes on and on, would all have had to just happen by pure chance, and in perfect synchronization, for the evolution theory to play out. Each of these, along with each step in the evolutionary chain, also carries with it staggering odds of occurring.

Astronomers have been searching diligently for any sign of life on other planets, but the conditions thereon have, as yet, yielded no chance of evidence of life. Only Earth, as far as we know, offers a life-sustaining atmosphere. So, the odds of even our existence are very slim.

Earth supports a water system, myriads of types of plant life designed to accommodate and feed myriads of creatures. The gasses, elements, soils, and water found here are extensive and essential for our survival. They even vary from one climate zone to another. The ecological balance here is amazing and astounding!

Now examine each and every step evolution would have to take from one celled water creature to diversified species of fish, crustaceans, and all of the various other fresh water and sea life. Then move on to amphibians in all their ranges. Land creatures follow, with countless species in the insect, fowl, mammal, and reptile groups. Then break each group down: for example, mammals can be aquatic or terrestrial; marsupial, egg-layer, live-birth, rodent, and so on. Bring to mind just a few diversified animals. Consider how intricately made every single one of these is, and how they interact with each other to form a balanced natural world. If all of this 'evolved' by chance, the probability chart must have imploded by weight of numbers!

Next, look at the highest form of evolution—the human body. How many different tasks can the human hand perform? It can clap, grasp, turn, hit, stroke, pat, pinch, punch, etc., and the list is practically infinite. How many colors can the eye perceive, not to mention depth, texture, distance, light, and dark? How many functions do the organs perform? What are the probabilities involved in the formations of the amazingly intricate workings of the nervous, circulatory, glandular, and reproductive systems? Carry this thought through with an inexhaustible number of other examples, and the conclusion is obvious. As a happenstance of chance, evolution must be limited to adaptation of a species to its surroundings only. As an explanation of our creation, it is not the right choice.

Life, then, had to be conceived by a very high intelligence, and in a very orderly and precise fashion. To create our world and everything in it, this intelligence must have superhuman qualities that our imaginations cannot possibly fathom. The only explanation is that this power, much greater than that of chance, did it. Therefore, God must exist.

2

Is He Loving?

Once it is established that God does exist, a whole host of concerns and questions usually ensue. The human soul needs reassurance. Did God sort of throw everything into existence and then sit back and let it all play out on its own? Does He care what happens to us collectively, or even more importantly, individually? Does He love us?

Think for a moment about the good things God has given us. He not only gave us perception, but vision; and not just vision, but vision expanded to perceive color, texture, and so on. This way, not only are we able to go far beyond mere perception for our own protection, we can also enjoy and appreciate beauty in its many forms with the gift of sight. That certainly is no evolutionary necessity. Mother nature, varieties of foods, the wonders of reproduction, and the five senses, while all necessary for survival, are enhanced for our pleasure. Scenic vistas, starry skies, balmy breezes, rich chocolate, smiles, laughs, puppies, and perfumes need never have been put on Earth, but they were. These are all marvelous gifts.

Gifts are given because someone cares, rather than by random selection. Love is the greatest gift of all. Without it, human beings shrivel up and die. Why is that, if it is not necessary for survival of the body? Instinct is definitely necessary, but is emotion? All of these extra 'perks' in life must be for a reason.

God must love us, then. If He loves us, He wants what is best for us. He wants us to be content. He wants us to be close to Him. He wants a relationship with us. He has our best interests at heart. He put everything in motion on Earth and in Heaven to fulfill all our needs and longings because of His generous, loving nature.

Since He is God, He is perfect. If He is perfect, so is His love. It is unconditional, without bias, and full of mercy. He can be trusted utterly and completely for everything, and He will never let us down!

3

Why do Bad Things Happen?

Certainly, bad things happen. The whole gamut of evil deeds and their consequences touches every single person on the planet. Disease, pestilence, famine, terrorism, abuse, and natural disaster all put fear into hearts worldwide as being beyond the human capacity to cope.

Did God cause all of these things? Why doesn't He do something to prevent them? If He loves us, why do bad things happen?

Surely, God wants us to love Him back, but sometimes when bad things happen, it seems natural to blame Him and difficult to love Him. We get it in our minds that He is mad at us for something we have done or not done. In fear or stubbornness, we then try and alienate ourselves from Him. However, God is totally merciful. He gave us the ability to conceive of Him and love Him. That would be improbable at best were He not loving Himself. His love is completely perfect, so there must be some other reason.

In order for us to have the capacity to love, we must make the decision to love. To make that decision, we must have free will. Otherwise, God would have a bunch of identical robots running around the earth, devoid of personality. Free will is what gives each person individuality. The old saying goes, "You are what you eat." In reality, you are what you decide to be. All kinds of factors play into it, but the bottom line is *you* make the determining decisions about yourself.

Because we have the gift of free will, many choose to abuse it. They decide to give in to their selfish desires and hurt others in the pr
Usually, they deny to themselves the existence of God, in ord
due and anesthetize their consciences.

That is not to say everyone who does not believe in God is wicked, but even the good ones tend to convince themselves that the world is one of relativism and shades of gray. In doing so, they unwittingly ignore the natural laws for people that God set in motion, the laws that give every individual value, dignity, and freedom. Instead, they choose other theories and philosophies that better suit their personal desires. When the rules are ignored, society becomes too permissive to accommodate all human beings' best interests.

Liberty and license are then confused. There is a huge difference between the two. Liberty allows for the equal pursuit of happiness of each individual within necessary parameters for the greater good. License is deceiving. It removes the parameters and makes the person believe he may do whatever he likes for self-gratification, with little regard for the consequences to others. It usually involves a rationalization process that relieves the conscience of its guilt, but still heaps, however unintentionally, bad will on those in the way. Or, it may seem innocuous at the time, but later on develops consequences. Either way, in the long run, innocents suffer.

Even good people, who want what is best for everyone, become confused by relativism and have great difficulty determining right from wrong. They reject those parameters set up by God for our protection, and embrace license rather than liberty. Thus, suffering ensues. When someone suffers at the hand of someone else, whether or not there was malicious intent, the latter has been disobedient to God and has committed sin.

In reality, we as human beings are not very good at determining right from wrong on our own and need guidelines to point us to these eternal truths. They are available to us if we just know where to look for them. If we seek God and all His Truth, the solutions are far less complicated and confusing.

There is another aspect to consider. Of course, other kinds of bad things happen, as well, those that are beyond our control. For example, natural disasters are completely non-discriminatory and wreak havoc randomly. We must go way back to the beginning of the creation story for an explanation of these.

4

From Sin Comes Death

Before sin, there were no diseases, pestilences, murders, or disasters of any kind. The first people had perfect communication with God. They actually spoke with and heard Him audibly. All creatures lived in perfect harmony. Life was immortal and delightful!

Who or what caused sin? Lucifer was God's most beautiful and prized angel until he decided he wanted things his way. Full of self-pride, he and several followers rebelled against God. This rebellion and disobedience created sin. In order to keep Paradise holy, God had no choice but to cast him and all his cohorts out. Adam and Eve, the world's first people, succumbed to his temptation, and Lucifer was given dominion over the earth.

Lucifer is now known as the fallen angel, Satan. His great pride continues to rule his actions. He is tremendously power-hungry and wants to wreak havoc wherever he can. Misery loves company and Satan wants all people in his camp. He is great at deception and confusion. He wants those shades of gray. Relativism is his ally. He does not care whether he is believed in or not, so long as God is not believed in either. He is the one who tempted Eve, and, as a result, became the author of all sin and suffering on Earth.

This caused a chain of events leading to corruption, decay, and ultimately, death. As chastisement for sin, God changed weather patterns and altered the land. It had to be worked to produce, and bodies had to be sustained. Childbirth became laborious and difficult. The aging process brought about the body's demise.

Later, the great flood wiped virtually every living creature from the face of the earth, with the exception of the inhabitants of the ark, in order to cleanse the world of sin. In another instance, the one universal language was divided many times over, and people no longer understood others'. They were scattered around the globe and had to survive harsh new environments. They were now necessarily vulnerable to the elements.

5

Why Would a Loving God Allow Sin?

Why did God allow sin to come into the world? This question has plagued mankind from the beginning of time. The best explanation goes back to free will. Without the ability to choose, there are no differences among us. It follows that without opposites, there are no choices. So, good as well as evil are necessary.

We cannot know joy without sorrow to show us the difference between the two. Neither can we understand kindness without cruelty. Light and dark, heat and cold, war and peace; the paradoxes are infinite and perplexing to us. Here is where faith steps in—faith in a mind greater than our own that has the perfect wisdom we finite beings cannot possibly fathom. This perfect wisdom allows things to play out that seem detrimental to us at the time, but which will ultimately lead to our happiness and salvation if we trust and obey.

Unfortunately, because every person is human, every person is subject to sin. No one is completely perfect and clean. We all have 'skeletons in our closets'. Since we are human and imperfect, not one of us is worthy to enter the Kingdom of God. Only He is holy enough for that!

Yet, God knows that the only way to keep Heaven pure for us is to allow no one into His Kingdom who *is* guilty of any sin. God will allow no imperfection for His children. If He did, then Heaven would be corrupt. He is perfectly holy and only perfect holiness can be allowed for the citizens of Heaven. Otherwise, the sin and death cycle would be repeated. This is completely unacceptable to God! He loves us too much to put us through that again, and He will never allow Satan any dominion of any kind in His refuge and paradise for His children.

So, how can He compromise these two conflicting facts? How, then, can we possibly expect to be accepted by Him, and allowed into Heaven? As impossible as it may seem, later you will see that He has a solution for us.

6

Why Did He Create Us?

God is all-sufficient unto Himself, meaning He does not **need** anything apart from Himself. In addition, He already knew from the beginning that life on Earth was not going to be a 'Garden of Eden', but rather involve sin, and therefore suffering. So, why did He create us?

Again, it was out of His tremendous love. He wanted to share with us all the unfathomable wonders of His Kingdom and Eternity. We are told that there is a paradise beyond our wildest imaginations waiting after this life. It is like Earth was originally intended to be, like the real Garden of Eden. God wants someone to share that with; someone who has the intelligence to fathom what a gift it is. It must be so wonderful, it is worth going through all the troubles in this life to attain it!

Just as adults do not need children, most have a great desire to have them anyway. They want someone with whom to share their lives, to teach, and to offer the wisdom of their own experiences and years. It is a natural outpouring of love. The instincts of parents to protect and nurture their children can only be explained by this unconditional love that permeates every aspect of their very lives. Even after the children have grown and left home, in most cases familial ties remain very strong. (Admittedly, some families are dysfunctional, but the term itself indicates a deviation from the norm.) The bond of family is an awesome force.

That is how close to us God feels. He created each individual and feels a fatherly love and devotion to one and all. We are His family. Indeed, He is more than a father; He is our all-in-all: father, brother, friend, and spouse. He can fill every void we experience. What is more, He wants to. That is how much He loves us. This love of His is unwavering and unconditional. All we need do is avail ourselves of it. Just like a good father, no matter the depravity of our lives, if we turn to Him in sincere repentance, He forgives **everything**. He has promised never to forsake or abandon us and He never goes back on a promise. That is how perfect He is!

Does that mean nothing bad will ever happen to us once we accept Him? It goes back to the free will issue, which leads to sin and suffering. So, while we are mortal, we are subject to the wages of sin. However, we do have the assurance that God will bring together for good **all** things for those who love Him, including the bad things. That is a most blessed assurance, even when we are too limited in understanding to see the good.

There are times when suffering is necessary for us to get His message. We all well know how much we take for granted when things go smoothly. Sometimes He allows bad things in order to get our attention. Once He has it, we are much more easily taught. When we learn what His will is for us, and submit to it, we are far better off in every way.

Of course, we would all rather have our lessons taught in a positive, pleasant way. Sometimes, miracles are His avenues to us. When a miracle works according to His purpose, (and remember, His purpose is divine and perfect,) then, certainly, we can expect to see one.

God wants only the best for His children and is completely just in all His actions. Only through our submission to His perfect will can His perfect love make our lives abundant and fulfilling. Only then, our cups can and do overflow.

7

Is God's Way Best?

If one must be perfect to get into Heaven, then every rule and commandment must be kept completely and utterly, right? But, all the rules cannot possibly all be kept to the last iota by any human being. Perfection is impossible. Sometimes it seems like God wants to keep us in a box and control our every move. So many things that seem pleasurable and innocuous are not allowed.

Remember that God made rules for our own good. He made them to give everyone equality and to protect us from our own sinful nature. He actually knows that by living by the rules we are happiest.

For example, we know that God hates divorce. Why is that? If two people are not happy together, why stay together? Ask any child that is the product of a broken home about his sense of security, well-being, and happiness. Check the statistics on these children with regard to educational performance, crime, out-of-wedlock pregnancy, drug abuse, and so on, and you will have your answer. What if no children are involved? Most people would rather not divorce if they could find a better solution. The bonds that exist in marriage wrench people apart, inside as well as out, when they are broken. Abuse, infidelity, selfishness, and neglect are the usual culprits that lead to divorce. They all take their toll on the human body and psyche. They are all against the rules.

How about extra-marital sex? Look at medical disease statistics regarding this topic. Then look at statistics regarding single parents and their children. They are negatively staggering. Education about safe sex has failed miserably at preventing disease and poverty. The statistics continue to climb, despite millions of dollars invested. Education will never supersede human nature. The rules were made for our protection.

The list goes on and on, but the principle is the same. If God's laws are obeyed, the world lives in harmony and peace. If not, people suffer. Therefore, the rules were not made to be domineering and tyrannical, but loving. We, as God's children, need His just discipline for our survival. What is more, His Will is that we not only survive, but also thrive!

That is why He told us the law is not just to be written in stone, but on our hearts. That is what gives us liberty. That is what keeps us out of the box. It takes away the burden of the law, and replaces it with the perfect spirit of the law. The most important law is to love God first, then each other as we would ourselves. If we do that, all other laws will be automatically obeyed in their true sense.

Will we be able to obey perfectly while on this earth? No, but God looks at our hearts and intentions, and has mercy on those whose wills are submitted and who truly love Him. Human beings will never achieve perfection, but we can grow closer to it by letting Perfection work through us. How and why God shows mercy will be explained in a later chapter, and they are integral to salvation. Together, they are the most precious gift any of us could wish to own.

8

Self-Esteem

What if you do not like God's plan? You think you have a better one. Why not let every religion into Heaven? Why not eliminate religion all together, so maybe people will stop fighting with each other?

Though it seems to make sense in earthly terms, it is pride on your part to assume you have a better plan than God's. You are second-guessing the Almighty Creator of the Universe.

God, we have established, is sovereign, just, and loving. He is also omnipotent, omnipresent, and omniscient. In other words, He sees the whole picture a whole lot more clearly than we do. He gave us instructions on how to live because He knows how we best function and are happiest. He also wants us in Heaven with Him, so He told us how to get there. His plan is superior to anything we can come up with. In fact, it is perfect because He is perfect. What is more, it is the only one that will work in the long run. It does not seem likely He will suddenly change his sovereign plan for the destiny of the whole world because you think you came up with a better one. He probably will not substitute the gospel according to *you* instead of His Holy Scriptures.

Remember, pride is what got Lucifer thrown out of Heaven. He thought he had a better plan, too. We have all taken pride in our talents and accomplishments. We struggle to be humble, because we compare ourselves to others and find personal superiority in many areas. What is important to us we strive to achieve, and take satisfaction in success when a goal comes to fruition. Often, we blind ourselves to our faults, or we see our good deeds as outweighing our bad.

We think we deserve good things because we have worked hard for them.

In reality, not one person on earth is perfect enough to be worthy or deserving of Heaven. We may excel in one area, but fall short in another. We are far inferior to the perfection needed. So, how do we truly come to the realization of this fact? How do we change our whole process of thinking?

The focus must move from oneself to God. This is a very humbling experience. The human ego, from a very early age, has taken precedence. A realization of one's insignificance and indebtedness must act as a catalyst to erase years of selfish thought processes. Every talent and strength we possess is a gift from God; every weakness allowed by Him for the sake of free will. We must come to terms with the fact that on our own we cannot possibly obey every rule to perfection. We are created to be individuals, each with strengths and weaknesses, and each subject to temptations.

Even the most saintly of us will sometimes err. This is why it is important never to compare oneself with others. God never compares. He looks at each person individually. Our contest is with our own individuality, not with our neighbor.

Where does that leave us in God's estimation? By our actions, we are hopelessly lost. On our own merit, we will never meet with His perfection standards. Were He not a God of love and mercy, we would all have to give up and accept a very dismal future.

Thank goodness, He does not only consider our deeds, but more importantly our mindset; that is, our estimation of Him. He takes into account how much we consider all He has done for us. How penitent are we for our misdeeds? How much do we want to please Him? How much of our lives, (which really belong to Him), do we want to share with Him? How much do we show forth His love to others and, indeed, put others before ourselves? How much do we love Him? The way our hearts answer these questions means far more in God's estimation than our material blunders.

9

What is One Person's Worth?

All gifts and talents come from God. The individual may claim no credit for natural, inborn traits. Of course, development of these gifts through hard work and practice is commendable. But the gift itself is just that—something free, gratuitous, and unearned. Recognizing one's inferiority and unworthiness could be downright depressing!

What, then, gives a person worth? How does one go about from day to day without wearing sackcloth and ashes; that is, without feeling lower than a worm? We must look to God for our self-worth. If He can love us despite our imperfections, then there must be something worthy in us, somehow, through what He has done in us and for us. We seek to know how God feels about us, by seeking to know what, if any, sacrifices He has made for us.

Gifts do indeed show love, but self-sacrifice is irrefutable proof. Where is such proof found? We must go to His way of communicating with us—to His revelation of Himself and His nature to us. We must go to Holy Scripture, the Bible.

In it, we find that He loves us so much that He allowed His only begotten Son to die for us. This is why God shows us mercy.

You and I cannot imagine sacrificing a child of our own for any purpose, let alone for the saving of people who never quite measure up to our expectations; for people who do not appreciate and reciprocate all we have done for them. Remember, He loves us ***unconditionally!*** Only this kind of love would allow such sacrificial giving.

Why was this necessary? If only perfection is permitted in Heaven, then there must be a substitute for each of us, because we are imperfect. We must ask that Perfect Substitute to take our place, and pay for our sins, so that we may be worthy of Heaven only through Him. We were once worthy only of destruction, but once we accept this marvelous gift, we have the grand inheritance of glory beyond our wildest imaginations in the next life. We are adopted as sons and daughters of the Almighty Creator of the Universe! Now He sees us as perfect and sinless, because He sees us only through His perfect and sinless Son. The Son is our one-way ticket to the everlasting presence of God! He took our sins on Himself and offered the only perfect sacrifice possible to atone for those sins. Nothing else will ever suffice.

The most righteous person in the world has no more chance of getting into Heaven than the greatest sinner without acknowledgement of the Son as his or her substitute. Only through Jesus Christ is perfection possible. Only perfection is allowed in Heaven. To receive this vicarious perfection, all you need do is ask with a genuinely humble and contrite heart.

Imagine! God now sees you as perfect! He has forgiven every sin. He has adopted you as His child. That makes you royalty! You are a prince or princess of the greatest kingdom in the universe! He has a cosmic purpose for your life. He created you for some grand task, perhaps not by the world's standards, but to help fulfill His perfect plan for History (His story) to play out. What could be more glorious? Your worth is in God—what He has given you, what He has done for you, and what He expects of you.

With your royal status comes responsibility. Remember, perfection is not expected of you in your own strength; you are already seen as perfect through the Son. However, your response to the Son's sacrifice for you is now willingness and desire to submit your own faulty will to His perfect one in order to fulfill His plan for your life.

How is that accomplished? How can we know what His will for us is? How can we keep our own desires from getting in the way? How can God make us worthy of salvation?

He does so by giving us another part of Himself. Once we accept the wonderful gift of Christ's death in our place, we receive the Baptism of the Holy Spirit, Who now dwells in each of us. He gives us the gift of Divine Love. If we listen to His still, small voice, He will guide our every footstep, every breath, and every move. He will care for our bodies, minds, souls, spirits, and the very number of hairs on our heads!

The Holy Spirit is the third person of the Holy Trinity. He is the Comforter and Conscience within us. We see now, that there is only one God, but He is manifested in three persons. The first is the Father, God the Creator; the second is the Son, Jesus the Messiah. This concept is difficult for us to understand, and is possibly best explained by comparing it to a flame. A flame is one thing, but it has three parts to it. Of course, there is the physical fire; but also integral to it are the light and heat. All three make up the substance of the flame. Each performs separate tasks. Each is always there as equal and necessary for its existence. The same is true of the Father, Son, and Holy Spirit. They all make up one Perfect God, the same yesterday, today, and tomorrow, always and forever.

He will not allow us to fall. If we should stumble, we need only stick our heads through the clouds (look directly at Him, leaving all worldly cares behind) and ask for His aid. He will not fail us ever. He has promised not to, and He never breaks a promise. He will not necessarily lift us out of trouble, as there may be a divine purpose in it, but He will see us through it. He will send legions of angels to battle Satan on our behalf.

He loves us far more than we are capable of loving even ourselves or those dearest to us. He is as close as our very breath. Only He can give the kind of love we have sought all our lives. His love for us is infinite, uncompromising, and unconditional. And we are worthy of it through His Son, our Savior Jesus Christ.

10

Is the Christian Faith the Right One?

How do we know that we have chosen the right faith to be in true fellowship with God? How do know we should not choose the Jewish, Moslem, Buddhist, Hindu, or some other faith? Certainly, they teach similar morals, values, and virtues, and many good people are included in their memberships.

The answer to this question is two-fold. It hinges on the Resurrection and prophecy. These two aspects make Christianity unique. No other religion can come close to claiming anything so magnificent or corroborative, with the exception of Judaism. Since Christianity is the culmination of Judaism, the two cannot really be compared. However, the same proof is needed for the Jew as for the Muslim, Buddhist, Hindu, or atheist. So, the following arguments still ring true in any case.

First of all, let no dispute remain as to the existence of the man called Jesus. Documentary proof authenticates this fact beyond the shadow of a doubt. There are about 640 ancient copies of documents that tell us that Homer lived. Plato, Aristotle, and Julius Caesar, lay claim to ten or fewer. Of the latter three, the time span between their actual lives and the writing of the copies varies from approximately 950 to 1,400 years. In Homer's case, it is not known. Copies of documents pertaining to the life of Jesus number about 14,000, and the earliest known to exist were written around 100 years after He died.[1] That

Homer, Plato, Aristotle, and Julius Caesar lived is never doubted. Neither should be the life of Jesus.

Jesus had a profound ministry and an unprecedented impact during His earthly life. Details of it can be found in the four gospels of the Holy Bible. We are chiefly concerned here with the events that took place during His last week on Earth. Briefly, Jesus rode into Jerusalem on a donkey on the Sunday preceding the Jewish celebration of Passover to the cheers of the crowd declaring Him the Messiah. Later, the people turned against Him and handed Him over to the Romans, who had Him crucified for claiming to be the King of the Jews, by their law a treasonable offense. He rose again three days after His death in fulfillment of the Scriptures, and appeared among His followers for forty days until He physically ascended into Heaven.

So, let us examine the Resurrection. If it never happened, neither is Jesus the Christ, for the proof of His claims rests solely on its occurrence.

How do we know if it really did happen? We must examine the eyewitnesses—the apostles and followers of Jesus. How did they behave before the event, and after? Did their actions remain the same, or did significant changes take place? Only drastic changes would prove the Resurrection did indeed occur.

The events leading up to and following Christ's crucifixion were fraught with chaos among the disciples and all the Jewish people. On the Sunday before Passover, Jesus rode triumphantly into Jerusalem on a donkey. People threw palm and olive branches before Him, singing His praises as King of the Jews. By Friday of the same week, only five days later, they had so turned against Him that they accused Him of blasphemy and handed Him over to the Romans, who crucified Him.

When Christ was arrested in the Garden of Gethsemane, the disciples ran to His aid, and one, Peter, in an attempt to rescue Jesus, cut off the ear of a slave with a sword. Jesus immediately restored the ear, with Peter and all the disciples as witnesses. The point is that Peter was totally convinced he was defending the Christ! Later, however, during

Jesus' trial, Peter was so frightened to be associated in any way with Christ that he denied he knew Him three times to strangers!

Before the crucifixion, Judas betrayed Jesus to the authorities for money. Afterward, realizing what a horrible thing he had done, he committed suicide.

During the course of these five days, Christ's followers scattered and went into hiding; fearful that the wrath, which had befallen the man they thought to be the Messiah, would also befall them by association. Only a few were known to be present at the crucifixion. Most were not to be found after the burial, until the following Sunday, when the time came to embalm the Lord's body according to Jewish custom.

Why would people who had dwelt with Jesus for years, people who had witnessed miracles beyond human comprehension—of changing water into wine, healing the hopelessly ill, feeding multitudes with a single boy's lunch, and raising the dead after four days in the tomb—suddenly lose heart and faith? Their fear of falling to the same fate as Jesus must have been immense. The witness of it must have been terrible beyond imagination. The circumstances of it must have overwhelmed their sensibilities with such trepidation that it temporarily erased their very knowledge that Jesus was and is the Son of God. It must have been impossible to imagine how the Messiah could allow Himself to be beaten, scourged, spat upon, nailed to a cross, and crucified!

Serious doubts arose among them as to the validity of Jesus' claims. The Jews expected the Messiah to come in triumph and glory. Prophecy from the Scriptures had given them this hope. (These are yet to be fulfilled at the Second Coming of Christ). But, there were other prophecies among the Scriptures that they chose not to warrant. These other prophecies were too terrible to consider as pertaining to their Savior, prophecies such as:

> *He was despised and forsaken of men, a man of sorrows, and acquainted with grief; and like one from whom men hide their face. He was despised, and we did not esteem Him.* **Is. 53:3**

Fulfilled in:

He came to His own, and those who were His own did not receive Him. **John 1:11**

But they cried out all together, saying "Away with this man, and release for us Barabbas!" **Luke 23:18**

Even my close friend, in whom I trusted, who ate my bread, has lifted up his heel against me. **Ps. 41:9**

Fulfilled in:

While He was still speaking, behold a multitude came, and the one called Judas, one of the twelve, was preceding them, and he approached Jesus to kiss Him. But Jesus said to him, "Judas, are you betraying the Son of Man with a kiss?"
Luke 22:37, 38

He was oppressed and He was afflicted, yet He did not open His mouth; like a lamb that is led to slaughter, and like a sheep that is silent before its shearers, so He did not open His mouth. **Is. 53:7**

Fulfilled in:

And Pilate was questioning Him again, saying, "Do you make not answer? See how many charges they bring against You!" But Jesus made no further answer; so that Pilate was amazed. **Mark 15:4**

Therefore, I will allot Him a portion with the great, and He will divide the booty with the strong; because He poured out Himself to death, and was numbered with the transgressors; yet He Himself bore the sin of many, and interceded for the transgressors. **Is. 53:12**

Fulfilled in:

And they crucified two robbers with Him, one on His right and one on His left. (And the scripture was fulfilled which say, "And He was numbered with transgressors.") **Mark 15:27**

See also, in order of fulfillment: **Is. 53:1** fulfilled in **John 12:37**; **Zech. 11:12** fulfilled in **Matt. 26:14, 15**; **Ps. 35:11** fulfilled in **Mark 14: 57, 58**; **Is. 50:6** fulfilled in **Matt. 26:67**; **Ps. 35:19** fulfilled in **John 15:24, 25**; **Is. 53:5** fulfilled in **Rom. 5:6, 8**; **Zech. 12:10** fulfilled in **John 20:27**; **Ps. 69:9** fulfilled in **Rom. 15:3**; **Ps. 109:4** fulfilled in **Luke 23:24**; **Ps. 22: 17, 18** fulfilled in **Matt.**

27:35, 36; Ps. 22:1 fulfilled in ***Matt. 27:46; Ps. 34:20*** fulfilled in ***John 19:32, 33, 36; Zech. 12:10*** fulfilled in ***John 19:34; Is. 53:9*** fulfilled in ***Matt. 27:57–60.***

The Open Bible lists forty-four fulfilled prophecies by Jesus in all referring to the Messiah. Those listed above refer to the suffering of the Messiah. Remember these prophecies were spoken hundreds of years before Christ lived, by people who were never to meet Him on Earth. Only God could have revealed these truths to them. Together with the others, they offer very convincing arguments for Jesus' fulfillment of them, and explain why His followers behaved as they did in the midst of them.

Because Christ died on Friday afternoon, just as the Sabbath was arriving (the Jewish day starts with sunset), He had to be buried quickly without the customary procedures. As the Jewish Sabbath holds strict dictates, which must be observed carefully, these procedures had to wait until Sunday morning. When Mary Magdalene went to Jesus' tomb at the prescribed time, she found the stone rolled aside and no body. Then, an 'angel' spoke to her in the cemetery. She soon recognized this angel as Christ Himself. When she told her story to the apostles, Peter and John ran and saw the empty tomb for themselves. Later, Jesus appeared to all His disciples in the flesh on several occasions during the course of forty days, at the end of which, He physically ascended to Heaven.

There are many theories that try to discredit the merit of the above-mentioned events, but only the veracity of this story would be enough to bring about the dramatic changes that took place among the disciples. It has been said, for instance, that the Resurrection was a big hoax created to perpetuate a false religion. People who do such things invariably do them for personal gain. Did the followers of Christ gain anything monetarily or otherwise? How did their lives fare afterward?

As was mentioned earlier, Judas Iscariot, who betrayed Jesus, committed suicide shortly afterward. He had gained monetarily, having been awarded thirty pieces of silver for the betrayal. What would have brought him to such utter despair that he killed himself? Only a stark and revolutionary personal enlightenment could have had such an impact; that is, the realization that he had sold out the Son of God!

History tells us that Andrew traveled to Greece and Russia to preach the Gospel, and was, it is believed, crucified by pagans. James was martyred by the sword, in Jerusalem, by King Herod Agrippa I. Philip is believed to have been crucified, head down, in Hierapolis, Greece. Tradition holds that Bartholomew traveled to India and then to Armenia where he was flayed alive. Thomas was purported to have been sold into slavery and sent to India, where, eventually, he was bludgeoned to death by soldiers. Matthew traveled to the East, where he was believed to have been martyred, circumstances unknown. James the Less (so-called perhaps because of his stature), author of the New Testament book, according to the historian Josephus, was stoned to death in the year 62 A. D. Thaddeus, or Jude, as he was sometimes called, author of the New Testament epistle, and Simon the Zealot are believed to have been martyred in Persia.

Peter, who had previously acknowledged Jesus as the Christ, whom Jesus had praised as having had revelation from God, who had witnessed the magnificent Transfiguration (Christ's transformation into a brilliant, heavenly appearance), and who had even walked on water himself at the Lord's bidding, suddenly lost all faith temporarily, and denied he knew Jesus three times! Christ had even warned him that he would do so, and Peter vehemently denied that he ever would. After the Resurrection and Ascension, however, he became one of the greatest evangelists of all, for the Jews and later the Gentiles. He traveled extensively for this purpose alone and spent the last years of his life as the Bishop of Rome. His earthly demise came at the hands of the Romans, on a cross. Tradition holds that he was crucified upside down because he did not feel worthy to die as the Savior had.

John the Apostle is the only one of the original twelve who is believed to have died of natural causes. He was present at the crucifixion and was asked by the Lord to care for Mary, His mother. John immediately took her as his own, and cared for her for the rest of her life. He was exiled for evangelizing to the island of Patmos as an old man, and was there given the Revelation of Jesus Christ, the last book of the Bible. He is believed to have died in Ephesus at the age of ninety-four.

The list goes on of disciples and followers who were miraculously changed following the Resurrection. The Apostle Paul never knew Christ in His lifetime and was even an emphatic persecutor of Christians, until his miraculous conversion on the Road to Damascus. For the rest of his life, Paul traveled throughout the Mediterranean region spreading the Good News of Jesus Christ. Finally, he was imprisoned and beheaded in Rome for this very reason.

What, other than the Resurrection itself, would cause all these people to behave so differently afterward? Certainly not a lie; no one would be willing to sacrifice the rest of his life, without hope of earthly gain, for such a thing. It goes against human nature to do so. Nor could they **all** have been crazy. There is far too much eyewitness testimony and evidence of changed lives to substantiate that notion.

There remains only one possibility. The Resurrection was a real event. Because of this, the story handed down by the apostles and others must be true. Therefore, Jesus was, is, and always will be the Messiah.

11

Our Destiny

What a blessed thought! Someone came down from Heaven to save us from ourselves! Someone was willing to stand in our place and suffer and die as payment for our sins. Someone, who was spotless and blameless Himself, the ultimate Sacrificial Lamb, loved us that much! He loves us still. His will is that not one of us should perish, but enjoy eternal bliss with Him.

It does not matter whatsoever what we have done, what we look like, or who we are. We are loved beyond our comprehension right now, as we are. What matters is this moment and henceforth.

Once we realize and acknowledge His great love for us, we are forever in His debt. All sense of pride is gone, for we know our gifts and talents come from Him alone. Through Him our sins are forgiven and forever forgotten, merely for asking with a truly contrite heart. We know we are not worthy to eat the crumbs under His table, but He is always merciful. What great love for Him, that creates in us, for He has taught us how to love through His Perfect Sacrifice for us.

Now we can gladly relinquish our selfish desires and live for Him! We have a new sense of purpose, far greater than anything we can imagine for ourselves. We know He has created each one of us for a portion of the fulfillment of His perfect will. We walk from henceforth in that knowledge, seeking to lead a new life and wanting to do His bidding. It is through us, His people, that His Church lives. Through us, His will is done. It is through us that others will know the saving grace that we enjoy. It is through us that the whole world may hear the most precious message ever. Finally, by the fulfillment of His plan through us, the Lord and Savior Jesus Christ will come back, in glory beyond our wildest dreams this time, to reign over all! He will give us a new and perfect world, one with no sickness, tears, or death!

We need not worry as to how we are to begin to accomplish such a feat as He has assigned us. He will do it through us, through His Holy Spirit. All we need do is surrender our will to His. We now know His is far better, and is the only way to achieve the utopia we all long for.

We are in His care forever. Nothing can touch us, in Heaven, on Earth, or below, that is not under His scrutiny. He will send legions of angels to protect us when in danger. We are now adopted sons and daughters of the King of the Universe. We are royalty! We belong to Him. We have communion with Him. He is ever as close to us as our very breath! Through all our trials, as long as we focus on Him, we will never fail. Though we may stumble, we will never fall. Through Him, we have the eternal victory!

We have come full circle and know why we are here. This is a marvelous and new discovery for us, but its Truth is eternal. There really is nothing new under the sun.

Epilogue

Every new believer has now inherited a precious gift; indeed, the most precious this life has to offer. Such a gift needs careful attention to remain pristine and perfect. It cannot merely be thrown in a closet, but must be polished and displayed. Many instructions are given in the Holy Bible for its upkeep.

Baptism is the sign of the New Covenant given to us by our Lord Jesus, and He instructs that, by it, we all be initiated as Christians. We are also taught to keep the Lord's Supper, so that we may dwell in Him and He in us. Thus, we remind ourselves of His immense and perfect sacrifice for us. Loving instructions for our benefit are contained in His Holy Word, so He asks us to study it diligently. He also asks us to have fellowship with believers for the edification of each to the other and thereby for His Beloved Church.

As we continue to grow spiritually, to pour out ourselves and take on the Holy Spirit instead, we will experience joy and peace unspeakable. No longer can the imperfections of this world touch our souls. We are under the protection of the Most High for all eternity, and a special place is reserved for us in Paradise! What a gift! What a blessing! What a wondrous God we serve!

Endnotes

1. Statistics taken from <u>New Testament Documents: Are They Reliable?</u> By F. F. Bruce.

0-595-28420-5